The Valley of Mist

Told and illustrated by Arcadio Lobato

KV-197-736

Floris Books

In a faraway land there was once a beautiful city. It lay hidden in a deep valley always covered in mist.
No one in the valley had ever climbed the mountain slopes to see what was beyond.

ACC. NO.		FUND
626737 06		JFI
LOC	CATEGORY	PRICE
ET	CC	8.99

12 JUL 2000

CLASS No.
J821.91 LOB

OXFORD BROOKES
UNIVERSITY LIBRARY

OXFORD BROOKES UNIVERSITY
LIBRARY   HARCOURT HILL

This book is to be returned on or before the last date stamped below.
A fine will levied on overdue books.
Books may be renewed by telephoning Oxford 488222
and quoting your borrower number.
You may not renew books that are reserved by another borrower.

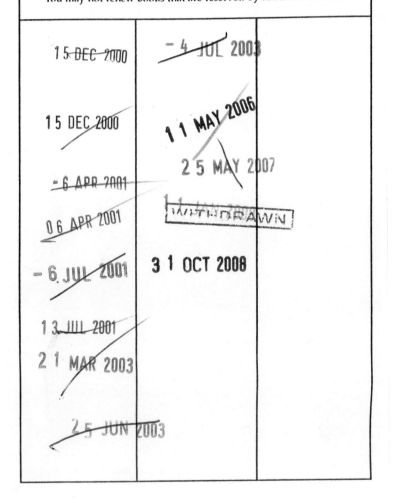

1 5 DEC 2000

15 DEC 2000

- 6 APR 2001

0 6 APR 2001

- 6 JUL 2001

1 3 JUL 2001

2 1 MAR 2003

2 5 JUN 2003

- 4 JUL 2003

1 1 MAY 2006

2 5 MAY 2007

WITHDRAWN

3 1 OCT 2008

OXFORD BROOKES
UNIVERSITY
LIBRARY

00 626737 06

Translated by Polly Lawson
First published in German as *Das Tal im Nebel*
© 1986 bohem press, Zürich, Switzerland
English version © 2000 by Floris Books, 15 Harrison Gardens, Edinburgh
British Library CIP Data available
ISBN 0-86315-312-7
Printed in Italy

The people there had never seen the sun shining in the sky above. The moon and the stars were unknown to them.

No traveller had ever come to tell them about these things.

The elders of the city said to the people, "Nothing could possibly be more beautiful than our valley, so there can be nothing outside."

The parents said to their children, "We have everything we need here. There is no need to search for anything else."

The children believed them, and when they grew up, they said the same to their children and grandchildren. And so years and centuries passed.

Just outside the city there lived an old man with his grandson.

When people passed by, they said, "Look, that's where Stefan lives with his foolish old grandfather."

For the old man had once declared that behind the mountains there was another world, shining and full of colour ...

Ever since then, the elders had called him a fool and banished him from the city.

His grandfather told Stefan, "I'm too old now to climb out of the valley again. Perhaps one day when you're big enough, you will find your way to the mountain-top and see the light shining, as I once did."

That night Stefan lay awake. He was so sure his grandfather was telling the truth, he wanted to prove it to everyone.

He decided to set off that very night to the mountain-top.

In the forest it was very dark, but Stefan carried on bravely. Through the trees, he heard the rushing river and an owl hooting and wolves howling.

He thought the river was saying, "Don't go on, it's a waste of time."

The owl in the tree seemed to be hooting, "There is nothing outside the valley."

The wolves seemed to be howling, "If you go on, you will die."

Stefan was very frightened, but still he walked on through the night.

As Stefan climbed, the mist became thinner and thinner.

At last, he found himself at the summit of the mountain, and for the first time in his life he watched the sun rising over the land, filling the world with light and colour.

From up here he could see how the clouds hung low, filling the valley. Only the very highest towers of the palace peeped out of the mist.

Stefan hurried back to the city and went to speak to the Council of Elders.

"I have seen a world full of light and colour beyond the mountain," he told them.

Someone cried, "Take no notice, it's only Stefan. He has gone mad like his grandfather!" Everyone laughed.

Stefan got angry. "But you can see it, too, from the top of the highest tower of the palace!"

"It is forbidden to climb the towers," the elders cried. "The rulers of old said it was dangerous. No one is allowed up there."

"Nonsense!" shouted Stefan as he ran to the doorway of the nearest tower and began to climb the steps. He was very quick on his feet and soon disappeared.

The elders leapt after him, crying, "Call the guard! Stop him!"

The guards chased up the steps after him. "Come back," they yelled, "or we'll lock you up in prison." The elders followed behind as fast as they could.

Stefan saw they couldn't catch him and he kept climbing up and up till he reached the very top of the tower.

When the guards and the elders arrived at the top and looked around, they cried out in surprise: "Ah! Oh! Ah! Oh!"

They were all full of amazement at the light and colour over the whole land. Stefan and his grandfather had been right after all.

Stefan ran straight home to find his grandfather, to tell him everything that had happened. His grandfather looked at him with pride and joy.

Then Stefan went and slept, because he was very tired after his adventure.

From that time on, the city began to send out its people to explore beyond the mountains. They learned about the sun-filled world out there. They discovered other cities and other people, and told them about their valley of mist.

Soon travellers came from far and wide to see the beauty of the city of mist.

High up on the mountain where the light and the mist meet, Stefan now lives with his grandfather in a little house.

And when people pass by these days, they stop and say, "Look, that's where Stefan lives with his wise old grandfather."